Never Hit a Ghost
with a Baseball Bat

Never Hit a Ghost with a Baseball Bat

Eth Clifford

*Interior illustrations
by George Hughes*

AN
APPLE
PAPERBACK

SCHOLASTIC INC.
New York Toronto London Auckland Sydney

ISBN 0-590-47784-6

Text copyright © 1993 by Eth Clifford Rosenberg. Interior illustrations copyright © 1993 by George Hughes. All rights reserved. Published by Scholastic Inc., 555 Broadway, New York, NY 10012, by arrangement with Houghton Mifflin Company. APPLE PAPERBACKS is a registered trademark of Scholastic Inc.

12 11 10 9 8 7 6 5 4 3 2 1   4 5 6 7 8 9/9

Printed in the U.S.A.   40

First Scholastic printing, July 1994

With respect and admiration for Zipporah—
good friend, loving daughter

Never Hit a Ghost with a Baseball Bat

Contents

•1•

Birthday Blues

Mary Rose Onetree was angry. She leaped into the front seat of the car and slammed the door hard. When her father stared at her, she looked away.

Her sister, Jo-Beth, was angry, too. She was already in the back seat. Her lips were set in a straight, hard line. She sat with her arms folded so tightly that her fingers left marks on her skin.

"Well," said their father, as he glanced from one to the other. "We're a happy little group, aren't we?"

"You can force me to go on this trip to wherever we're going." Mary Rose's face was stony; her fingers were gripped in her lap. She spoke without looking at her father. "But I am not going to enjoy myself," she threatened.

1

"She's mad because she wanted to go to Amy Beck's house just so she could see Amy's brother Jordan. She's in love with him," Jo-Beth explained. "Even though she hates Amy," she added.

"Amy Beck happens to be my very best friend in the whole world," Mary Rose snapped. "And for your information, Jo-Beth, eleven-year-old girls do not fall in love. Dumb old thing," she muttered.

Jo-Beth's eyes widened in surprise. "But you always said you hated Amy Beck. You said she was stuck-up and selfish and — "

"That was last month. Don't you know anything at all? Honestly!"

Mr. Onetree studied his daughter's flushed face. "I remember, when I was eleven . . ." he began.

Mary Rose held back a groan and slid down in her seat. Why did grown-ups always tell you what they did or said or thought when they were your age?

Before her father could go on, she said in an impatient voice, "Daddy, that was hundreds of years ago."

Her father allowed a small smile to appear

and quickly disappear. He started again, "Hundreds of years ago, when I was eleven, I had a mad crush on a girl named . . ." He stopped to search his memory. "Alice? Annabelle? No, Angelina. That was her name. Angelina something or other. I thought she was so beautiful, with her red hair that curled around her pretty face, and blue eyes so deep I wanted to drown in them."

"Daddy!" Jo-Beth wriggled with embarrassment. Sometimes her father got mushy with their mother, kissing the tip of her nose, or calling her Princess or his Golden Girl. Stuff like that. Grown-ups could be rather silly, she thought.

Mr. Onetree turned to grin at her. "Angelina couldn't see me for sour apples. She broke my heart. I wanted to die. For a couple of weeks, anyway."

"And then what happened?" Mary Rose couldn't help being curious. Jordan Beck was as mean to her as the long-ago Angelina had been to her father. Jordan Beck acted as if Mary Rose didn't exist. If he did notice her, he pretended not to know her name.

"Yes, Daddy. What happened?" Jo-Beth

was eager to know.

Mr. Onetree winked at her. "I got interested in trading baseball cards. Now, you've
told me about Mary Rose's problem. I'm not
starting the car until I know what's bothering
you, Jo-Beth."

Jo-Beth was not one to keep her emotions
bottled up for long. "I'll tell you," she said at
once. "I was eight years old yesterday. Eight!
And you know what happened?"

"The world came to an end?" her father
suggested.

"If you're going to make fun of me —"

"No. I'm not. That wasn't fair of me, Jo-Beth. I apologize."

"I had to go to *school,* just like it was an ordinary day."

Mary Rose turned around to stare at her sister. They looked somewhat alike, with their fine, straight brown hair and dark brown eyes. But Mary Rose's face seemed to be changing. She looked more grown up. And she sounded a little more grown up now, most of the time.

"Of course you had to go to school," she told Jo-Beth. "Everybody has to, even on a birthday."

"Is that a law or something?" Jo-Beth wanted to know.

If it was, she would change it someday. Her eyes took on a dreamy look.

Someday Jo-Beth would marry a prince. No, a king. That way she could be queen right away. Then she would pass a law. No one would be allowed to go to school or work on her birthday. It would be a national holiday. Flags would fly; parades would strut by; presents would come pouring in from everywhere.

5

"Hurrah for good Queen Jo-Beth," the people would shout.

She would be especially kind and gracious, even to Mary Rose and Harry Two, who at age six months now cried buckets just because he was teething.

She was shaken from her dream by the silence in the car. It pressed in on her ears. When she opened her eyes, she saw her father and sister staring at her.

Mary Rose said, "It's not as if we've forgotten. You're having a party tomorrow."

"No, wait. I think there's more to it than that. Am I right, Jo-Beth? Do you want to tell us about it?"

Jo-Beth started to speak, then she decided against it. They wouldn't understand at all.

Yesterday morning she had leaped out of bed just as the sun splintered the darkness of the night in the east. She had dashed to the mirror and studied her image. She was eight! She had waited a whole year to be eight. The face that stared back at her looked exactly as it had the night before. Nothing had changed! Her hair hadn't curled. Her eyes hadn't turned blue. No sprinkle of magic dust had turned her into Cinderella at the ball. She was still just plain old Jo-Beth.

Mary Rose had caught her at the mirror.

"I bet I know what you're thinking," she had said in that superior voice she used. "You and your imagination. I bet you thought you'd turn into the Snow Queen. Or that you'd grow wings and fly like Peter Pan. Or something."

"Don't be so childish, Mary Rose."

Jo-Beth had stalked past her sister with her head held high.

And here she was, Jo-Beth told herself, stuck in this car with her father and sister, on the way to who knew where.

As if Mary Rose could read her mind, she now asked, "Where are we going, anyway?"

"It's a surprise."

Jo-Beth sat up straight. "A surprise?" she repeated. "A birthday surprise?"

"In a way, I suppose. And I'm sure you'll both be delighted."

"Are we going straight there, Daddy?"

"Of course," he replied.

The two girls looked at each other and nodded, as if they shared the same thought. Of course? There was no such thing for Mr. One-

7

tree, whom their mother called Spur-of-the-Moment Harry. He wrote a column for a newspaper and claimed he needed to get out and see people and investigate new places as he drove along. A few of those spur-of-the-moment side trips had had some unexpected results.

"Can you at least tell us where *there* is?" Mary Beth wanted to know.

"Uh-uh. Can't. You have to wait and see. But I guarantee it will be different."

Different! That was what worried Mary Rose.

Different! Jo-Beth sat up, eager all at once for the trip to begin.

Different meant a new adventure, didn't it?

Jo-Beth sank back in her seat, her eyes aglow. Whatever it was, she was ready for it.

•2•

You Have Been Warned

Their father surprised them. He didn't dash off the main highway onto some interesting side road but drove straight on at a steady fifty miles an hour.

There were stops, though, along the way. Jo-Beth always had an urgent need to go to the bathroom whenever she was in the car for a long while. Mary Rose hated gas station bathrooms and used them with great reluctance.

"I probably have the world's record for holding my nose," she announced as she fled outdoors, closely followed by Jo-Beth. "I hate when you make us stop like this."

"You made us stop once, too," her sister was quick to point out.

"Stopping for food isn't real stopping. It's a necessity."

Jo-Beth grinned. "So is this."

Mary Rose ignored the comment, just walked back to the car with great dignity. "She's such a *child*," she complained to her father.

Jo-Beth made a face. "Look who thinks she's all grown up."

Mary Rose's expression was scornful. "I *am* practically grown up. I'm just past eleven. In two years, I'll be a teenager."

It was unfair, Jo-Beth thought. First no one had made a fuss about her birthday. And Mary Rose would be a teenager years before her. No matter how fast she grew older, she would never catch up with Mary Rose.

Both girls seated themselves in the car with grim faces.

Mr. Onetree had had enough. "If you girls don't lighten up . . ." His voice trailed off.

"You'll what, Daddy?" Mary Rose sounded hopeful. "You'll turn around and take us home?"

What a wonderful prospect. Maybe there

would still be time to go to Amy Beck's house. Maybe Jordan would smile, and say, "Hi, Mary Rose. You want to go to Freddie's for an ice cream soda?" instead of throwing her a blank look and a "Yo, kid. How's it going?"

"Absolutely not." Mr. Onetree was quite firm about that. "You girls will thank me before the day is over. Mary Rose, we're almost there. Take a look at the map."

He was proud of the way she could read a road map, proud he could depend on her for sensible and accurate directions.

"Look for Blair Road. We take the next right after that."

When Mary Rose bent her head to study the map, Jo-Beth shrieked, "We just passed it, Daddy."

She had an eagle eye when it came to road signs. She was always first to spot them, especially if they were the least bit unusual. She was in luck once more.

"Daddy! That sign. It says *Trolley Tracks to Bygone Days.*"

Mary Rose shook her head. "Not again," she sighed. "Not another one of Jo-Beth's signs." She crossed her fingers on both hands and made a wish. Nothing helped. Her father turned in just past the sign.

It seemed to the girls that the road would go on for mile after weary mile, but at last they spied a huge structure straight ahead.

Mary Rose sat up straight. "That looks like a hangar. For airplanes," she explained to Jo-Beth.

Jo-Beth began to bounce on her seat, her eyes bright and expectant. "That's it, isn't it, Daddy? You're going to take us for a ride in a helicopter. I've wanted to go on a helicopter ride all my life," she added, although the idea had never occurred to her until this moment.

Mr. Onetree smiled. "Nope. No plane ride."

Mary Rose could see how disappointed her sister was. She turned to her father. "I don't think that's asking too much. A helicopter ride would only take a few minutes. If it costs a lot, I have some money saved up — "

"You don't understand," her father interrupted.

By this time, they had stopped in front of the hangar. A tall, burly man with thick gray hair and a wisp of a gray-black beard hurried toward them. He stuck a large, powerful hand through the open window.

"I'm Stan Thorne. Glad you could make it, Onetree," he said.

Mr. Onetree beamed. "The owner of Trolley Tracks."

"The one and only," the man agreed.

"I can't see why we can't take one teensy little helicopter ride," Jo-Beth complained.

Mr. Thorne looked puzzled. "Helicopter?" he repeated. "There are no helicopters here."

"But this hangar," Mary Rose pointed out.

"Don't you have bunches of airplanes in there?" Jo-Beth wanted to know.

"Why, honey," Mr. Thorne said. "Didn't you understand my sign? This is a trolley car museum."

"A museum," Mary Rose echoed. She glared at her sister as if it was Jo-Beth's fault. Then she added, unfairly, "You and your museums."

"You and your Jordan Beck," Jo-Beth flashed back. She poked her father's shoulder. "What kind of a birthday present is a trolley car museum?" She was close to tears.

"Now don't jump to conclusions," he replied. He opened the door, stood beside Mr.

Thorne, then walked toward the hangar with him. The girls ran to catch up, but neither one looked at each other nor said a single word.

Once inside, they were overwhelmed. As far as the eye could see, in every direction, were trolley cars: small trolleys, huge trolleys. Open cars and closed cars. Double-deckers. Cars with curtains. Cars with women's names, like Althea and Rebecca and Pauline.

Mr. Onetree whistled in amazement. "I've never seen a collection like this. It must have taken you years."

"My dad started it . . . what, honey?" he asked when Jo-Beth spoke.

"Those iron stairs that are all twisty going round and round and up and up . . ."

He smiled. "They lead to my apartment. I live up there."

"In a museum?" Mary Rose glanced around. "Doesn't it get kind of spooky at night?"

"Creaks and noises and maybe a kind of whistling-wind-through-the-cracks kind of spooky?" His laugh boomed and echoed back.

"I only believe in things I can see, touch, smell, or feel, honey."

Just then an elderly man, dressed in a dark blue uniform trimmed with silver buttons, came up to them. He put his forefinger up to his dark blue cap in a quick salute.

"Here's Hoot, my all-around man here. Meet the Onetrees, Hoot."

"My pleasure," he muttered, though the small scowl that turned his eyes squinty told them it was no pleasure at all.

Thorne slapped him on the back. "Hoot is mighty possessive about the museum. He was a trolley car motorman way back. I have an idea. While Mr. Onetree and I have our interview, Hoot, why don't you show these young ladies around?"

As they watched their father and the museum owner go round about on the steps, all three were silent. Then Hoot said, "Name is Turner. Hoot Turner. Come on. I'll show you around."

Jo-Beth was curious. "Why would anybody want to collect trolley cars?" She said it as though she meant dinosaurs.

Hoot swung around to stare at her. "Why? History, that's why. Stories. People. Olden days. Golden times. That's why."

He marched off a little way, then turned back. "You might as well come along. I want to make one stop first."

He led the way to a rather long trolley, which seemed quite dingy and worn. Like the others, it sat on tracks that went nowhere. When he turned to caution them about the steps, he nodded his head toward the car. "She's not much to look at, but you come back next year. She'll be shiny and bright as a new penny."

The girls followed him inside, then stopped to stare all around in amazement. At one end of the trolley was a sofa bed with a wall lamp leaning over it as if about to fall. In front of the sofa, a long table held magazines stacked in neat piles. In the center was another table and one chair. A medium-size refrigerator stood beside a two-burner electric stove.

"It looks like somebody lives here," Mary Rose said.

Hoot Turner didn't answer, just pointed to

himself. "You girls like to have some milk and doughnuts?" he began as he pulled open the refrigerator door. He peered inside, pushed some items front and back, then turned and barked at them. "All right. Who stole my doughnuts and milk?"

Mary Rose and Jo-Beth stepped back.

He slammed the door shut and turned his attention to the table. "All right," he demanded, "what's going on here?"

Jo-Beth grabbed her sister's hand and held it so tight that Mary Rose winced.

"What's wrong?" Mary Rose tried to sound brave.

"You ask me what's wrong. I'll tell you, young lady. When I left here this morning to go on my rounds, I left dirty dishes on that table. I left my magazines all over the place. I was going to clean up later," he said, as if Mary Rose had accused him of sloppiness.

"But you did clean it," Jo-Beth said in a small voice. "Everything here is as neat as a pin."

That was her mother's favorite expression. She'd look around at the girls' rooms, get a stern look in her eye, and say, "I want these rooms neat as a pin when I come back, understood?"

"Maybe Mr. Thorne cleaned it up." Mary Rose offered what she thought was a logical explanation.

"Sam Thorne? The boss? Have you got buttons for brains? Oh, hey, I'm sorry," he said, when he finally noticed how the two girls stared at him. "I had no call to talk to you young ladies that way. I just keep getting riled, see?"

"No, we don't see," Mary Rose spoke right up. Jo-Beth was proud of her. Mary Rose could be a tiger, sometimes, especially when she stood up for her rights.

"It's just that strange things have been happening around here lately."

Jo-Beth's ears perked up. "Like how, strange? Like scary strange?"

"You said a mouthful, missie. Things disappearing. Trolleys made spick-and-span. And then there are the sounds. Ghosts, that's what it is. Ghosts of the past haunting this place."

"There's no such things as ghosts," Mary Rose announced.

"No? Then who cleaned up this place? Who

stole my milk and doughnuts?"

Jo-Beth was scared, but she couldn't help giggling. "Mr. Turner — "

"Hoot."

"Hoot, Ghosts can't eat. They don't have bodies."

"And they don't have hands, either. Even if they did, they wouldn't be strong enough to pick up dishes." Mary Rose sounded defiant.

Jo-Beth admired her sister. Mary Rose was so brave, so dependable. She made you feel safe.

"Mary Rose is right — " Jo-Beth began, and stopped in midsentence.

A voice, high, thin, wavering, made the fine hairs on her arm stand at attention.

"Beware," it called, stretching the word so Jo-Beth could almost see the letters spread out in thin wisps. "H — o — o — t. H — o — o — t. You have been warned. B — e — w — a — r — e."

•3•

How Do You Wrap a Ghost?

Hoot Turner took a deep breath. He pressed his lips together so hard they seemed to disappear into his mouth.

"I don't like this place." Jo-Beth shuddered. "I don't want a ghost for a birthday present."

Mary Rose gave her a sharp glance. "You're so ridiculous. You can't give a ghost to anybody. How would you wrap up a ghost for a birthday present, anyway?"

Jo-Beth closed her eyes. How would you wrap a ghost? Throw an invisible net over it, then tie it with an invisible bow? Even though she was frightened, she wanted to giggle.

Mary Rose noticed Jo-Beth's closed eyes but went on just the same. "There are no such things as ghosts, and that's that."

"Oh yes there are," Jo-Beth contradicted. "I've seen ghosts — "

"Ghosts on television don't count. Ghosts in books don't count." Mary Rose was quite firm about that.

Hoot Turner shook his head. Then he told Mary Rose, "Sister, when a voice out of nowhere calls you by name and gives you a warning, you better watch out."

Before he could go on, Jo-Beth grabbed her sister's arm. "Let's go find Daddy. I want to go home this minute."

"Shhh," Hoot Turner hissed. He turned his head to the right and listened. He turned his head to the left and listened.

The girls turned their heads, too. An awful silence filled the immense hangar.

"What do you hear?" Jo-Beth asked, her eyes fearful.

"Nothing. Not a sound," he said. He glanced at the two girls, who studied him with wide, worried eyes. He made a small chuckling sound. "Listen to me, will you? I must be getting old. That was no ghost. Just the wind whistling through this big barn of a place. Big, quiet places with not a living soul around except for me and the boss, of course — well, they get to you after a while. Know what I mean? I guess I let my imagination run away with me."

Jo-Beth stared at him in wonder. Imagination made him hear a voice? She couldn't believe it. No matter how hard she imagined things, no one spoke to her. Certainly not a ghost that said 'B — e — w — a — r — e.' *Especially* not a ghost that said 'beware.'

"Okay," Jo-Beth agreed at once. "It was the wind. Can we go get my father now?"

Hoot Turner sounded apologetic. "Now, little lady, Mr. Thorne said I was to show you girls around, and I always listen to the boss. What will he think if I bring you both back, scared silly with some weird story about a ghost? I'm sorry I got you girls all worked up over nothing. Let's look around, okay? I promise you'll find this place real interesting. And just think, you can tell your friends you were here even before the museum opened. How about that?"

He didn't wait for an answer. "First off, let's go to this next trolley."

"Do we have to?" Jo-Beth whispered to her

sister, but Mary Rose had already followed Hoot Turner. Jo-Beth went after them with great reluctance.

The trolley car was completely open on both sides. Rows upon rows of hard wooden seats lined each side.

The girls stared in delight. Seated on the benches were . . .

"Dolls!" Jo-Beth exclaimed. "I mean dummies. Like the ones in department store windows."

"Mannikins," Mary Rose corrected.

Jo-Beth gave a small sigh of exasperation. Why did Mary Rose have to be such a know-it-all?

"There are lady dummies, too. I mean mannikins. No, I guess I mean ladykins," she said. "And boykins and girlkins and babykins." She grinned at Mary Rose, who just made a face, then turned to Hoot Turner.

"Why did he want mannikins — " she threw Jo-Beth a furious look — "in here? Won't they be kind of scary to visitors to the museum?"

"Oh no. See, Mr. Thorne wants visitors to

get some idea of what it was like, back in the late 1890s. See? Everyone is dressed the way they did then. Even the kids."

Something caught Jo-Beth's eye. She walked quickly to the back of the trolley, turned, and called, "Not everyone. These mannikins are bare naked."

"Don't be ridiculous," Hoot Turner snapped. "All the mannikins have . . ." He broke off and stared. His face turned red. "Now who did that?" he barked.

Mary Rose, who had joined them, spoke up at once in her sister's defense. "Why are you asking us? We've never even been in a trolley museum before."

Hoot Turner scratched his head, then ran his hand over his face, squashing his nose to one side as he did so.

"If there's one thing I hate," he said angrily, "it's mysterious goings-on."

"Let's get out of here." Mary Rose was uncomfortable. Mysterious goings-on? Not for her, thank you just the same.

But Jo-Beth wasn't uncomfortable. The mannikins fascinated her. She walked back toward the front of the trolley, stopping here and there to examine them more closely.

"They're all smiling. They look so happy. From the way they're arranged, you'd think they were real families. See, Mary Rose? Some of the manni —— I mean ladykins, are holding babies."

Mary Rose ignored her sister. "Why are they so happy?" she asked Hoot Turner. "It makes you feel good just to look at them."

Hoot Turner couldn't help smiling as well. "This was a special car provided by the trolley company. All these people were going to a park set up by the company — "

"Like going on a special bus tour," Mary Rose interrupted.

"Right. The park had rides for the little ones, picnic areas . . . the kids played all kinds of games — one-foot races, baseball. You name it. Going there, some of the young men might play a banjo."

"What's a banjo?" Jo-Beth wanted to know.

Hoot Turner went to one of the figures and removed an instrument from its hands. He began to strum his fingers along the strings.

Some of the strings were missing, and the banjo was badly out of tune, so Hoot Turner replaced it in the mannikin's hands. Then he pointed to another instrument.

"You girls know what this is, don't you?"

"A guitar," they said together.

"Well, going to the park, the banjo was the right thing to play, all tinkly and jazzy. Coming home, when everyone was tired, and the kids were sleepy and worn out, one or two or more gentlemen would strum the guitar and sing soft, sweet songs."

Mary Rose sighed. "That's so romantic."

Jo-Beth studied her sister. Was sensible, down-to-earth Mary Rose imagining herself on a trolley, with dumb old Jordan Beck serenading her with a soft, sweet song? *Jordan Beck?* The boy who never used more than two words in a sentence? Catch Jo-Beth going sappy over someone like that.

"See?" Hoot Turner's voice broke into Jo-Beth's thoughts. "This man had a baseball bat."

He took the club, posed as if he was up at bat, then swung it.

"CRRR-ACK!" he shouted. "That's a home run."

Just then a voice boomed from a loudspeaker.

"Hoot. Thorne here. Mr. Onetree would like to see your collection of canceled trolley passes. Let the little girls wander around by themselves. They'll be fine. Get here on the double, Hoot. Thorne out."

Hoot Turner was thunderstruck. "Your daddy wants to see my collection. Nobody's asked to see them in years." He took a deep breath. "Imagine that. Say, listen. I've got to run back to my place. Here." He thrust the baseball bat into Jo-Beth's hands. He grinned. "In case you meet a ghost. Just swat it with this."

He tore out of the trolley. They could hear his footsteps echoing on the hard cement.

The girls stared at each other. Jo-Beth held the bat in a tight grasp.

She had to swallow hard before she could speak.

"He wants me to hit a *ghost*? With a baseball bat?"

28

"You're so silly. There are no ghosts. How many times do I have to tell you that?" Mary Rose was impatient. "And even if there was a ghost, how would you hit him? The bat would go right through him."

"That's right," said a voice from nowhere. "Never hit a ghost with a baseball bat."

Jo-Beth shrieked, and Mary Rose jumped.

Is Mary Rose's heart beating as fast as mine is right now? Jo-Beth wondered. One quick glance at her sister showed that Mary Rose was just as frightened as she was.

When she could find her voice, Jo-Beth whispered, "Who said that?"

Mary Rose looked all around cautiously. "I don't know," she began to whisper back and stopped short when the voice spoke again.

"Never ever hit a ghost with a baseball bat. Not ever."

Jo-Beth's feet began to take her almost automatically to the exit, but Mary Rose grabbed her.

"Who's saying that? Or are you afraid to show us who you are?"

Jo-Beth was overwhelmed by her sister's

courage. Here she was, ready to jump out of her skin while her brave sister was prepared to argue with a ghost.

"I'm saying that. Here I am. Over here."

Though the girls circled with care, they could see no one.

Then Jo-Beth licked her lips, which had gone suddenly dry, and said, "Mary Rose. Don't look now. But I think it's coming from that teddy bear. The one that little girl — I mean, girlkin, is holding."

"Teddy bears don't talk," Mary Rose announced. "Stuffed animals do not talk."

"Yes, they do, Mary Rose. Remember my doll, Baby Crystal? When I pulled a string, she said 'I love you' and 'I'm hungry' and 'I'm sleepy.' Things like that."

Mary Rose marched to the bear, snatched it from the mannikin's grasp, and examined it closely.

"There are no strings on this bear," she announced. "It's just an old, beat-up teddy bear that's ready for the trash can."

"Oh," said the bear. He sobbed, in little, short, gasping breaths. "How would you like it if I said that about you?"

"I'm getting out of here," Jo-Beth shouted. Mary Rose fled after her, still clutching the bear, as if she wanted to drop it but didn't know how.

"I want Daddy," Jo-Beth said in her best no-nonsense voice. "NOW."

Mary Rose had second thoughts.

"No," she said in a firm voice. "I said I don't believe in ghosts. If I run away now, I'll never know if they really exist. You can go back to Daddy if you want to. Just give me that base-ball bat. I'm going to find out what's going on around here even if — " She stopped and drew a long breath. "Even if it's the last thing I ever do."

Jo-Beth looked back to where the iron steps curled round and round. They seemed miles away. No way was she going to cover that distance alone.

"I'll help you, Mary Rose," she said bravely. But she couldn't help wondering if this would be the last thing she would ever do, too.

•4•

They're Alive!

"What are we going to do first?" Jo-Beth asked.

Mary Rose was uncertain. True, she had said she was going to find out what was happening. But where should she begin?

That was a puzzle, and she was almost sorry now she had been so positive. Then she pulled back her shoulders, lifted her chin, turned to her sister, and said with determination, "We'll have to search all the trolleys."

Jo-Beth was staggered.

Search all the trolleys? She looked left and right, then all around. All she could see was a vast area covered with trolleys.

Search them? *All* of them?

Jo-Beth sighed. "Do you know how long

that would take us?" she demanded. "About a skillion years, that's how long."

Mary Rose was annoyed. "There's no such word as *skillion*. Why do you always exaggerate everything?"

"Me? I've never exaggerated anything in my whole life," Jo-Beth defended herself. When she saw the expression on her sister's face, she added, "Well, maybe one or two teeny weeny exaggerations."

Mary Rose didn't answer. She was thinking hard.

Jo-Beth waited a moment, then asked impatiently, "How do we start looking for a ghost, anyway?"

The two girls stared at each other.

How did one look for a ghost? Wait for something to shimmer and glow? Look for a ghastly white presence? Listen for a wailing, eerie voice? A laugh that turned your blood cold?

Or wait to see a chair moving by itself, a pillow tossed in the air?

When Jo-Beth asked these questions aloud, Mary Rose shuddered. The same thoughts had occurred to her.

Was she about to change into a Jo-Beth?

Never, she told herself firmly. One person with too much imagination in the family was enough. She wondered briefly if Harry Two would take after Jo-Beth and their father, or be practical, like Mary Rose and their mother.

She realized she had been quiet long enough now to worry Jo-Beth, who looked both baffled and frightened.

"Listen, Jo-Beth. Just do whatever I do, okay?"

Jo-Beth nodded. But she promised herself that if they did find a ghost, she would scream loud enough to wake the dead. Then she would faint. She didn't know what people did exactly when they fainted, but she had seen enough movies and TV to understand that it was best to close one's eyes first. Maybe, though, she would roll her eyes around in her head before fainting.

That should prove to Mary Rose that a little eight-year-old child should not be on a ghost hunt.

That would show her father that it was a big mistake to take his daughter to a museum for her birthday. He would feel even worse when she told him bravely that she would forgive him.

Mary Rose interrupted her thoughts by announcing, "We might as well start with this next trolley. Then we'll just take them one by one as we go along."

"That's all right for you to say," Jo-Beth flashed back. "*You* have the baseball bat."

Mary Rose looked at her hand in surprise. She had forgotten all about the bat. Then she realized she also held the teddy bear.

"I think I should keep the bat for now," she replied. "If we do come across the ghost, I'm taller and stronger than you. I could hit harder. Why don't you take the teddy bear?"

Jo-Beth backed away. "Me? Take a teddy that *talks?* And *cries?*"

Mary Rose was fresh out of patience.

"Then I'll go in by myself and you can wait out here."

"I can't wait out here all by myself," Jo-Beth wailed.

Mary Rose's face grew stormy. "I've had it up to here with you," she shouted.

Jo-Beth stared at her sister. She looked exactly like their mother when she said that.

Even the gesture when she said "up to here" was the same, a sharp slash with her hand under her chin. That usually happened when Mary Rose and Jo-Beth were quarreling, and Harry Two was crying, and something was burning on the stove.

"Okay." Jo-Beth's voice was weak. "Let's go in."

But now that she had agreed, she felt as if her feet had become rooted in the cement floor. Should she go in ahead of Mary Rose? How could she? Suppose something was there, *waiting*. She had better follow Mary Rose. But that was just as bad. Suppose something suddenly came up behind her?

She had a change of heart. "I don't want to go in first or last or anything. I hate these trolleys. I hate this museum. I want to find Daddy and go home this minute."

Mary Rose felt a moment of sympathy for her sister. On the other hand, she couldn't stand not being able to solve a puzzle. So at last Mary Rose shouted, "I'll go in by myself."

She moved quickly up the steps and to the entrance. Then she stopped with a gasp.

Terror whispered to Jo-Beth: "Run for your life."

Curiosity urged her: "She found the ghost. A real live ghost. You have to see what it looks like."

Jo-Beth went to join Mary Rose, with hands clamped into tight, painful fists but her eyes shining and eager. She bumped into her sister, who stood frozen in place, nothing moving as she studied the inside of a trolley.

Jo-Beth couldn't believe what she saw, either.

This trolley was furnished like someone's living room. Large red velvet easy chairs were placed in small groups, with small marble-topped tables in between. In the center were two red velvet–covered benches, separated by what seemed to be a low, quilted headboard. At the far end was a piano. Heavy velvet drapes were held away from the windows with long, twisted cords.

What had startled the girls, however, were the figures.

Men sat in the easy chairs. One held an unlit cigar in his fingers. Another read a newspaper, his glasses perched at the end of his nose. Four were playing cards. And still another was seated at the piano.

"Mannikins," Mary Rose whispered, as if they could hear her.

Jo-Beth knew they couldn't speak or hear. Still they seemed so real she expected that at any minute one of them would raise his head and bark, "What are you kids doing here?"

She stepped back. She didn't like this uneasy feeling.

"We better get out of here, Mary Rose." She spoke in a low voice, as if afraid she might be overheard. "This is really spooky."

Mary Rose didn't seem to hear her. She was fascinated. "I wonder if that piano is real," she said to herself.

She made a quick decision.

"Here." She thrust the bat and bear at her sister. "Hold these while I go look."

Jo-Beth was horrified. She had automatically held out her hands for the bat and bear. Now her heartbeat thrummed in her ears in a rapid rat-tat-tat. She didn't mind the bat, but the bear — what if it began to talk again?

"Wait, Mary Rose," she cried. "Don't leave the bear with me."

But Mary Rose was already heading for the piano.

Jo-Beth called after her with an anxious warning. "You better come back. They don't want us here. Can't you tell?"

Mary Rose called back, "I just want to take a quick look, that's all. And mannikins don't have feelings."

By this time she was already at the other end of the trolley. She studied the mannikin at the piano. He had his head tilted, as if listening to the tune he was playing. His eyes shone; his lips were parted in a small, contented smile.

Mary Rose ran her fingers up and down the keyboard. It was a real piano, but it made no sound. Then she noticed a small lever and pressed it.

The piano sprang to life. The keys went up and down in rapid motion — black keys, white keys, all the keys from one end of the keyboard to the other.

Mary Rose was so startled, she sprang back. As she did so, she knocked over the mannikin on the bench. "Oh, I'm sorry," she gasped.

"I'm so sorry. Did I hurt you?"

From the other end of the trolley came a wail of fear from Jo-Beth. "He moved. He moved. I told you. He's alive. They're all alive."

It wasn't her imagination. Hadn't the man with the newspaper lowered it to glare at Mary Rose? Hadn't the four men stopped playing cards and turned their heads to stare at Mary Rose?

"We're doomed," Jo-Beth told herself. It was one of her favorite expressions. Their father would come looking for them and find their still, lifeless bodies. And no one would ever know . . .

"Whatever you're thinking, forget it," Mary Rose yelled. She knew how Jo-Beth's imagination went into full speed. She was furious with herself, so of course she had to blame her sister.

She had apologized to a mannikin, which was exactly the sort of thing Jo-Beth would do. Dumb, dumb, dumb, she scolded herself as, pale and shaken, she seated the mannikin back on the bench.

When she rejoined Jo-Beth, she was still irritated. " 'They're alive. They're alive.' Is that all you can say? You and your imagination. They're dummies, dummy. The only people alive are you and me. What are you so afraid of, anyway? You have the baseball bat, remember? Use it if somebody moves."

Jo-Beth looked down at the baseball bat in her hand. She had forgotten it was there. She had the bear, too. But suppose the bear had decided to talk while Mary Rose was at the other end of the trolley? She didn't want to think about that.

When Mary Rose saw how pitiful her sister looked, and how small somehow, she put her arms around her. She often quarreled with Jo-Beth, particularly when Jo-Beth was impossible — moody and stubborn and uncooperative. This time, however, Jo-Beth was right. It had been frightening — the sudden burst of music, Mary Rose's gesture that knocked over the mannikin and made it seem, for a moment only, to have moved by itself.

She needs me to take care of her, Mary Rose thought to herself. This was a good time to be kind.

"I was scared, too," she admitted. "But I guess it will all look different when the tourists come. There will be lots of talking and laughing and kids running around. Then these displays won't look so weird. It will just be a look back into the long ago, to see how it used to be in the olden days."

Jo-Beth felt comforted, but she was still uneasy. "It's like being in a wax museum," she grumbled.

Mary Rose contradicted her. "Oh no it isn't. Wax museums are gory-scary."

She shivered, remembering a trip with her class to a wax museum. She had had nightmares for weeks.

Jo-Beth looked all around. "Isn't this scary enough for you? Mannikins that look like real people, and voices out of nowhere, and toy bears that talk and cry?"

"It's mostly because this is such a big place, and so empty. Of real people, I mean," Mary Rose added. "Daddy and Mr. Thorne are real people. I could scream. I'm a really good screamer. They'd be down here in a minute. They can save us, Mary Rose."

Mary Rose could feel her blood freezing in her veins. Jo-Beth had screamed in the Haunted House once. Just remembering it made Mary Rose shudder. The *Indianapolis News* described it as "Pandemonium Erupts in Haunted House. Goblins Flee."

She clapped her hand over Jo-Beth's mouth. "Don't you dare scream. Anyway, we can't yell for Daddy. You know the rule when he's working."

Jo-Beth nodded. Her father could be lots of fun, warm and understanding. But not when he was working. Never when he was working.

Their mother had once explained, "When your father is writing, he has no family and no friends."

So Mary Rose was right. As usual.

It must be wonderful to be like her, Jo-Beth thought, able to reason things out in such a calm manner. Well, maybe when she was older she would be different, not so emotional and so easily scared by her own imagination.

She guessed she really had been rather silly, and too quick to panic. Just the same, she ran ahead of Mary Rose, eager to leave the trolley. Mary Rose, pondering what to do next, walked with eyes cast downward. So, at first, when she joined her sister, she was not aware that something was wrong. Then she noticed that Jo-Beth stood frozen, staring past her.

Not again, she told herself with a sigh. What was Jo-Beth dreaming up now? Still, there was something about the way Jo-Beth looked . . .

Mary Rose turned, very slowly.

Jo-Beth opened her mouth in a silent scream.

Mary Rose turned to stone.

A mannikin stood several yards away, its eyes burning with anger.

•5•

Dirty, Rotten Crooks

For one long awful moment, silence lay heavy between them. The girls were in shock; the mannikin remained motionless.

At last Jo-Beth swallowed, took a deep breath, and asked, "Are you a ghost?"

Mary Rose turned to her sister and said, surprised, "I can't believe you said that. Does it look like a ghost? It's just a mannikin. Mannikins are not ghosts."

Jo-Beth wondered how Mary Rose always had such positive knowledge. How did *she* know, anyway? Ghosts could be anything they wanted to be. They certainly would not get an argument from Jo-Beth. She did feel, however, that she had to correct Mary Rose about one thing.

"It's not a mannikin," she pointed out. "It's

a boykin. We saw boykins on the trolley that went to the park, remember?"

It was indeed a boykin, dressed like the others they had seen, in a blue shirt with a round white collar, a black string tie that formed a loose bow, and short pants. Although the girls didn't know it, these pants were called knickers. Long black stockings and tightly laced black shoes and a round-brimmed straw hat completed the costume.

This boykin looked exactly like all the other child mannikins they had seen, except for one thing. This one wasn't smiling. Its eyes were wide and angry. And then it spoke, in a high, reedy, tremulous voice.

"You stole my teddy!" it accused Jo-Beth. "You're mean and you're a crook — "

Mary Rose sprang to her sister's defense. "Nobody stole your teddy. We found it — "

Jo-Beth interrupted. She had come to a swift conclusion. "You're not dead," she cried. "You're alive." She turned with blazing eyes to Mary Rose, and shouted, "You never *listen*. I told you and told you they were alive. But you didn't believe me. Well, what do you say now?"

Before Mary Rose could reply, the manni-

kin said, "Of course I'm alive. I've been alive all my life. Are you alive?"

"Of course I am. But I've never been a boykin that's a dummy — "

The boykin was furious. "I am not dumb. I'm five years old, and I know lots and lots of things. George Washington was the first president of the United States. Did you know that? I bet you didn't. I'm only five and I know that. And I know something else. You're both crooks. You give me back my teddy."

Mary Rose had opened her mouth a number of times to interrupt but couldn't get a word in. Jo-Beth had simply stared at the boykin.

Then, suddenly, the teddy bear began to cry. In between little hiccups of sobs, it wailed, "You did so steal me. I don't like you. You give me back."

Jo-Beth jumped back in alarm. With a feeling of panic, she held the stuffed animal as far away as her outstretched arm could reach.

Mary Rose was startled, too, but she was also suspicious. She glared at the boykin.

"How did you do that?" she demanded.

"Never mind!" Jo-Beth could feel goose

bumps banging into each other up and down her arms. "Here's your dumb old teddy bear. I never wanted it in the first place."

She hurled it away from her as hard as she could. It landed almost at the boykin's feet. Immediately he stooped, swept it up, and hugged it close. Then he held it away and scolded it.

"I told you not to run away. I told you and told you. See what happened? Dirty, rotten crooks stole you."

Mary Rose was furious. "Who are you calling a dirty, rotten crook?"

She stepped closer to the boykin, who began to look frightened.

"There's something very peculiar going on around here," she went on. "I want to know what it is. I want to know who you are and why you're dressed like that, and . . . and . . ."

The boykin drew back, clearly afraid of her now. Clutching the teddy bear, he turned and fled.

"Wait!" Mary Rose shouted.

But it was too late. The boykin had disappeared around a trolley and was gone.

"Oh no you don't," Mary Rose yelled. "You

just wait till I get my hands on you."

She ran, and Jo-Beth followed reluctantly. She hated her sister when she dug in her heels this way. What made her so stubborn? Who cared where the boykin went so long as he just stayed away for good? Why couldn't Mary Rose ever leave well enough alone?

"There he is. We've got him now." Mary Rose sounded triumphant. "I knew we'd get him."

She was mistaken. The boykin, visible for the moment, vanished once more.

Jo-Beth stopped abruptly.

"I want to go home. Right now." Her voice was weepy, the way it always sounded when she was truly miserable.

"Come on, Jo-Beth, I don't want him to get away. Let's keep after him. I want to find out who he is and what he's doing here."

Jo-Beth shook her head. "You can chase him if you want to. Not me."

Mary Rose shook her head in disbelief. "Are you telling me you don't want to know what's going on around here? Aren't you even a little bit curious?"

"No, Mary Rose. I'm not curious. I'm just

plain scared and uncomfortable and I want to find Daddy and go home and I never want to go to another museum again in my whole life, not even when I'm married and have children and they want to go to a museum."

Jo-Beth paused, gulped air, and went on again nonstop.

"And if Daddy doesn't come soon, I'll just hold my breath till I turn blue and die and then everybody will be sorry, especially Daddy, and I'm eight years old and I didn't have a happy birthday."

Mary Rose stared at her in amazement. The words had exploded from her sister like fizz from a soda pop can after it's been shaken hard.

"All right," Mary Rose agreed after a moment of silence. She was reluctant to give in to Jo-Beth's spasm of speech. She hated not solving this puzzle, but she did feel responsible for Jo-Beth.

And maybe, she told herself, Jo-Beth felt things more deeply because of her overactive imagination. When they saw a scary movie, Jo-Beth would be up all night, terrified by her dreams, while Mary Rose slept peacefully.

"Okay, Jo-Beth," she said, her voice kindly and understanding. "Let's go find Daddy."

"Which way do we go?" Jo-Beth asked.

Mary Rose stared at her sister. "Which way? Don't be silly, Jo-Beth. We just . . ." Her voice trailed off. Which way *did* they go? In chasing after the boykin, Mary Rose had lost her sense of direction. They were trapped in a maze of trolleys.

Jo-Beth waited. She studied her sister's face. "You don't know, do you? Mary Rose! You don't *know*. We're doomed. We'll turn into mannikins and people will come and stare at us and never know we were real people once upon a time."

"Don't *do* that," Mary Rose stormed. She stopped to think hard, worrying her lower lip. Jo-Beth immediately felt more hopeful. Whenever her sister twisted her lip, she somehow came up with a solution. At last, Mary Rose's eyes brightened. "Okay. Here's what we'll do. We'll just keep walking in one direction. Sooner or later, we'll hit one of the walls of the building. Then we'll work our way around the building along the wall . . ."

It took a short while, but the plan worked.

Once they reached the wall, they were able to see the winding stairway.

"We're saved. We're saved. Let's go get Daddy, Mary Rose."

"Wait, Jo-Beth. We'll have to go back."

"Go back? Go *back*?" Jo-Beth couldn't believe it. "Why would we do something dumb like that?"

"I still have the baseball bat. It doesn't belong to us," Mary Rose explained. "All I want to do is put it back where it belongs. And you don't have to worry. I'll know the way back again now."

Jo-Beth didn't want to be unreasonable. She also didn't want anyone else to call her a dirty, rotten crook.

"Okay," she agreed. "But then we'll go find Daddy, right?"

"Right."

Jo-Beth sighed with relief. Wait till they told their father about this place. He wouldn't be so eager to write about it then. He would just march them out straight to the car. Maybe on the way home they would stop for a treat. We deserve a treat, maybe a double-rich chocolate cake drowning in whipped cream, with lots of nuts . . . Her mouth began to water in anticipation.

"You know what, Mary Rose," she began but stopped short. She had just caught a glimpse of something. Should she tell Mary Rose? No, better not. It was too late.

Mary Rose had seen her expression change. She glanced ahead. It was then that she saw what Jo-Beth hesitated to reveal.

The boykin and his teddy bear had reappeared, then darted into a trolley ahead, and disappeared once more.

·6·

Are You a Friend of the Family?

"Quick, Jo-Beth." Mary Rose gave her sister a triumphant smile. "We've got him. Come on. This time he won't get away."

As she chased after the boykin, she muttered under her breath, "Now we've really got you. And you're going to talk. Oh yes you are."

She could feel that warm glow of satisfaction that came when she was at last in control. It was how she reacted when she finished a difficult jigsaw puzzle, or solved a math problem that had given her a hard time.

Jo-Beth pounded after her. She, too, muttered under her breath. But her thoughts were not at all like her sister's.

I'm only going to be eight years old one

time in my whole entire life and what am I doing? I'm chasing a boykin and his dumb old teddy bear, getting scared out of my socks, and my hair turning gray . . .

She liked the sound of that. Eight years old with gray hair. No, not gray. White. Snow white. And lots and lots of wrinkles.

People would look at her with sidelong glances, and whisper to each other, "She must have had a terrible tragedy in her life."

Jo-Beth nodded. She liked the sound of that, too. A terrible tragedy. She wouldn't speak, of course. Not a word would pass her lips. She would just hold her head high and look brave . . .

By this time she had caught up to Mary Rose. As she ran the length of the trolley, she noticed a single printed word that sent a shock of dread through her.

"Mary Rose," she called, in a strangled voice.

But did Mary Rose listen? When did Mary Rose ever listen?

Mary Rose had already walked through the entrance to the trolley. She came to such an abrupt halt that Jo-Beth ran into her. She snatched at Mary Rose's sleeve and uttered one word.

"Hearse." The word was a raven's croak.

Mary Rose didn't need to hear that word. What she saw was more than enough to send a cold shiver up and down her spine.

A mannikin, dressed in a black suit, faced her from just a few feet away. Along a bench on one side of the trolley were four other mannikins. At the far end, a closed coffin rested on a stand.

Jo-Beth inched forward, fascinated in spite of her fear. As she did so, she stepped on a metal plate on the floor. The plate moved under her feet.

At once, a number of things happened.

The most mournful music ever played on an organ filled the air.

The mannikin in the black suit bowed his head. He clasped his hands in a sorrowful gesture. His eyes were sad. And then he spoke in a hushed voice.

"Are you a friend of the family?"

"No," Jo-Beth was apologetic. "I'm sorry . . . ouch! Why did you pinch me, Mary Rose? That hurt."

"You're *talking* to it."

Jo-Beth's hand flew to her mouth. Mary Rose was right. Jo-Beth had apologized to a dummy. The mannikin had spoken, and she had actually replied.

Mary Rose had been about to say something else but stopped when she caught sight of movement among the mourners on the bench.

An elderly mannikin with gray hair drawn back into a tight knot had pressed a handkerchief to her lips. Next to her, a young woman with wide blue eyes and fair hair seemed to glance toward them with surprise. The third was a girlkin who studied her shoes with a grim expression. The fourth was a man who held a hat in his hands as if about to turn it round and round.

"Mary Rose." Jo-Beth's voice was low but urgent. "This is a hearse. It said so outside on the trolley. This is a funeral."

"It can't be," Mary Rose whispered. She was stunned. Her eyes were fixed on the scene. Jo-Beth was right for once in her life. This was a funeral. She started to inch backward. Then she changed her mind.

Sure it looked real. But it just didn't make sense.

Their mother had told Jo-Beth any number of times, "It's all right to imagine things. But you have to be sure you know the difference between what you imagine and what is real."

"In other words," their father had added. "It's okay to have your head in the clouds as long as you have both feet on the ground."

Well, Mary Rose knew the difference. None of this was real.

Mannikins did not die, so of course there was no body in the coffin.

Mannikins didn't feel, so of course they couldn't cry.

Mannikins did *not* ask you if you were a friend of the family, because mannikins did not have families.

This time Mary Rose moved toward the coffin at the other end with a purposeful air.

"Mary Rose," Jo-Beth wailed. "That's not the way out."

As Mary Rose kept walking, Jo-Beth called in disbelief, "Are you going to the coffin?"

Poor Mary Rose, Jo-Beth thought. It's been too much for her. She's lost her mind. I'd better get her out of here.

Jo-Beth inched up to her side. "It's all right, dear," she said, trying to sound like their mother when she soothed Harry Two after a fall. "Come with me. I'll take you out. Don't worry."

Mary Rose glared at her. "This is all fake. Every bit of it. And I'm going to prove it."

"How? How are you going to prove it, Mary Rose?"

"I'm going to open that coffin this minute.

And you know what we'll find?"

Jo-Beth closed her eyes.

What would they find? Dracula? Godzilla?

"I don't want to know," Jo-Beth said.

Mary Rose shook her head. "I can imagine what you're thinking. Well, you can relax. Because I know exactly what we'll find. Nothing."

"Nothing?" Jo-Beth was suddenly hopeful.

Of course. Her sister was so clever. It was wonderful how Mary Rose could think things through all the time.

Jo-Beth could visualize what would happen next.

The coffin would be empty. Naturally. Nobody in his right mind would go around burying a mannikin.

Then there would be nothing more for Mary Rose to prove. They would leave this dismal trolley, and as soon as they were outside, Jo-Beth would show her sister how firm she could be when she had had enough.

She would announce in her most positive voice, "Okay. This is it. Baseball bat or no baseball bat, I'm going to find Daddy. You can come if you want to. But I don't care. I'm not stepping foot in another one of these trolleys."

She might even add, "Not today. Not ever."

"Okay," Jo-Beth said aloud. "Let's go." Then she noticed with horror that Mary Rose had her hand on the lid of the coffin. She struggled with it briefly, then ordered, "Help me."

"Help you? *Help* you?" Jo-Beth repeated. "*Me?*"

"No. I'll ask old Mr. Friend of the Family to help. What are you afraid of, anyway? I told you the coffin is empty."

"I believe you. Honestly, Mary Rose. I do. If it's empty, why do we have to open it? I don't like opening coffins," Jo-Beth sobbed. "I'm not supposed to open coffins. I'm too little."

Mary Rose grabbed her sister's hand and put it on the lid.

"Now." Her face was grim. "When I say lift, you lift."

At that moment, a voice wailed, "Help! Get me out of here. I can't breathe. Help!"

The girls were paralyzed.

That eerie voice most certainly was coming from inside the coffin.

·7·

Are There *Two* of Them?

If Jo-Beth could have grown wings, she would have flown away. Without a backward glance, she would have abandoned Mary Rose, still glued to the coffin. She would have left her father to his interview. What she would do was head for home like an arrow to a bull's-eye.

But she couldn't grow wings. And though her brain sent a sharp message to her legs, *RUN*, her legs refused to respond.

Maybe the next best thing was to scream loud and long. Her voice, however, failed her.

Mary Rose had been busy with her own thoughts. She told her sister, "That did it. Now I *will* open this coffin."

She had that determined gleam in her eyes that meant she would worry at this puzzle the way a dog worried a bone.

"Help me, Jo-Beth. On the count of three, let's push as hard as we can."

Jo-Beth shook her head. It went back and forth, back and forth. Her head said no; her thumping heart said no.

"Not me," she said. "You can count to a hundred if you want . . ."

Mary Rose ignored this. She did her countdown slowly — three . . . two . . . *one*.

Jo-Beth's hands were on the lid. When Mary Rose said *one*, she pulled. Together, they managed to lift the lid. It moved upward in slow motion.

The girls stared, mouths open. Then Jo-Beth caught her breath. Mary Rose bit her lip in anger.

"I knew it," she said. "I just knew it. It was just a trick."

"It's a mean, scary trick." Jo-Beth was fighting mad. "Just you wait till we find that boykin . . ."

Mary Rose looked again, as if she still couldn't believe what she had first seen.

The boykin's shabby, worn teddy bear seemed to fix her with its button brown eyes.

Mary Rose made a decision. She reached down and lifted the teddy bear. Then she threatened, "If that little monster wants this bear back this time, he'll have to answer a lot of questions first."

Jo-Beth moved a few steps away. She knew the bear was just a small, stuffed animal. She knew it wasn't alive. But she didn't trust it anyway.

As they began to leave the trolley, careful not to step on the metal plate, Jo-Beth was struck by a sudden thought.

"Mary Rose, how did that boykin put the bear into the coffin? It took both of us to lift the lid."

Mary Rose came to an abrupt stop. She studied her sister as if she couldn't believe what a sensible question she had asked.

"You're right," she said, after a moment. "You're absolutely right. That little monster couldn't have lifted the lid. Do you know what that means?"

Jo-Beth didn't want to know. But who could stop Mary Rose from telling her?

"It means," Mary Rose went on, "that some-one is helping him."

Jo-Beth felt a cold shiver start at the top of her head and work itself down to the tip of her toes.

Someone else?

Two of them?

"I'm out of this place," Jo-Beth said. "This time I'm really going to get Daddy. And I don't care if we never give that miserable baseball bat back."

Mary Rose had forgotten she still had the bat. She had put it down to lift the coffin lid. Then, when she grabbed the bear, she automatically picked up the bat as well. She gave the bat a brief glance. She was still at work on the puzzle. She spoke her thoughts aloud.

"So. There are two of them. But one of them has to be bigger and older. Two little monsters couldn't have raised the lid. No way. All right. We'll just have to find both of them, wherever they are."

Jo-Beth refused to answer. She marched straight ahead, her eyes fixed on the far end of the hangar. If she could make it past all those cars and across that vast stretch, she would be safe. She would leave this place forever, and ghosts and mannikins who came to life could scare somebody else.

Mary Rose seemed to awaken from her deep concentration. When she noticed the expression on her sister's face, she felt a twinge of guilt. After all, Jo-Beth wasn't having a great birthday.

"Okay, Jo-Beth. You're right. Let's . . ." She broke off in midsentence. She forgot all about her sister's woe. Instead, she skidded to a halt. "Jo-Beth! There he is! I just saw him scoot into that trolley."

"I don't care if he scoots into a million trolleys. You want to go after him, go ahead. I'm going to find Daddy, Mary Rose. And don't you try to stop me."

Mary Rose paid no attention. She raced toward the trolley into which the boykin had disappeared. Soon she, too, vanished into the car.

Jo-Beth was surrounded by an acre of silence. She was alone, absolutely, totally alone. Her imagination ran riot.

What would she do if . . . no, she didn't want to think about that. But suppose . . . no, no, *no.*

There was only one thing to do. Find Mary

Rose. Mary Rose was brave. Mary Rose was smart.

Jo-Beth flew to the car ahead, climbed in, and stood still.

Mary Rose was in the center of the car, hands on her hips, her eyes bright. When she heard her sister behind her, she put a finger to her lips.

"Shhhh!" she cautioned.

Jo-Beth didn't need to be warned. She couldn't have spoken at that moment, no matter what.

·8·

Hide and Seek

"Do you believe this?" Mary Rose asked at last. "This is weird, really weird."

At the back of this trolley, a huge scarecrow stretched from floor to ceiling. A jacket covered the top part, or tried to, for straw burst through, and the one button in the center seemed about to pop. Faded jeans and overlarge sneakers completed the costume. The head was the largest pumpkin the girls had ever seen.

"He's looking right at us," Jo-Beth said.

"Pumpkins don't look. They have no eyes. And even if they did, they couldn't see, because the eyes wouldn't be real."

How did Mary Rose do it, Jo-Beth wondered. How could she always come up with a reasonable explanation? Of course, she didn't believe in dragons or monsters or aliens . . .

"You get scared," Jo-Beth accused. "I know you do."

"Sure I do," came Mary Rose's quick reply. "But I know I'm only looking at something made up, or reading something pretend. I don't get all shivery when I go to sleep and climb into your bed the way you do in mine."

"I'm only a little kid," Jo-Beth pointed out.

Jo-Beth used that as a handy excuse quite often.

"Well, maybe the scarecrow isn't really looking at us," Jo-Beth went on. "But the witches are."

Near the scarecrow, three witches sat around a black stove, huddled together as if they plotted some mischief. All clutched straw brooms with ragged edges. It seemed as if they would fly off as soon as their conference was over.

Toward the center, four witch children were seated at a table. Small chalkboards were in front of each one. They held long white pieces of chalk in their hands.

The girls edged closer to see if anything was written on the chalkboards.

"They're doing their homework." Jo-Beth was enchanted with the idea. "I didn't know witches had to go to school."

She peered at a word scrawled across the top of the board, then said it aloud in a puzzled voice. "*Witchmatic?* What's that?"

"One and one is two. Two and two is four," Mary Rose explained. "Only this witch," she pointed to the figure nearest to them, "has to solve a problem. See?"

Jo-Beth leaned over and shook her head. Mary Rose recited: "*If it takes thirty minutes for three witches to fly across the full moon on Halloween, how many children can they frighten in ten minutes?*"

"I hate those kind of problems," Jo-Beth said, but Mary Rose paid no attention. She had already moved on to the next board.

"This one is doing spelling." She laughed. "Listen. It says '*Correct the spelling in this sentence: Witch weigh can a which way a which?*' I bet you can't do it, Jo-Beth."

"That's easy." Jo-Beth took the chalk and

wrote in a quick hand, *Which way can a witch weigh a witch?*

She beamed. "I'm the best speller in my class."

Funny how relaxed she felt now. It was all supposed to be so scary, but this was the most relaxed time she'd had since they had come to this museum. She looked all around, then told her sister, "You know what? I like this trolley. It's kind of fun. A little bit scary but nice, just like it is on Halloween," Jo-Beth said.

She gazed at the black cats with hunched backs and lips parted in snarls and smiled.

She touched one or two pumpkin heads with lopsided grins which were lined up around the scarecrow.

"You know what?" Jo-Beth said. "It would be really scary if they moved. I wonder if we can get them to do that."

She glanced all around, certain there must be a way. Then she spotted the metal plate on the floor. Without a word to Mary Rose, who seemed to be lost in thought, she went and stepped on the plate.

Instantly, there was action. Orange lights

beamed from the eyes of the scarecrow. They flickered on and off and made the huge figure look threatening.

The witches around the black stove turned and stared. Then they cackled. They slitted their eyes and moved their brooms.

The small witches began to sing in shrill voices that made the girls wince.

"School days, school days.
    Forget the golden rule days.
    Screeching and frightening
    And witchmatic
    Taught to the tune of a
    Large broomstick . . ."

Without warning, all motion and sound stopped. The orange eyes of the scarecrow became blank. The witches froze, their brooms still held high.

"Why did you turn it off, Mary Rose?" Jo-Beth was exasperated. "I wasn't scared . . ."

Her words trailed off as she saw her sister's expression. She licked her lips, which had become dry.

"You didn't, did you?" she asked in a shaky whisper.

Mary Rose didn't reply.

Jo-Beth watched with eyes wide in surprise as her sister began a slow, thorough search of the trolley. She peered behind the witches and even peeked under their long black skirts. She went from seat to seat and brushed her hand beneath them in a long, sweeping motion. She then dusted her hands by brushing them against each other.

Finally, she went to the scarecrow and punched it smack in its middle. Some loose straw flew out and settled on her hair.

Jo-Beth found she could speak again.

"What are you doing?"

"What do you think I'm doing? Playing hide and seek, only somebody is hiding and I'm going to seek until I find him. Or them," she added, remembering her suspicions.

"You think that boykin is in here someplace . . ."

Mary Rose nodded. "Looking for that stupid teddy bear . . ." She clapped a hand to her mouth. "The teddy bear. What did I do with it?"

"I saw it on one of the seats along with the baseball bat when I came in," Jo-Beth said.

Both girls ran to the entrance. They searched every seat.

The teddy bear and the baseball bat were gone.

•9•

A River of Popcorn

Jo-Beth was glad.

"Good," she said. "Now we're rid of that dumb old teddy bear. And we don't have to worry anymore about putting the baseball bat back. So let's get out of here, okay?"

Mary Rose was furious. "No, it's not okay. Somebody is playing games with us, and I'd like to find out who. And why," she added. "Why are they picking on us? What did we ever do to them?"

Mary Rose didn't expect an answer, but Jo-Beth replied anyway. "Maybe they don't like us being here."

"Why not?"

Jo-Beth shook her head. She didn't know why not. After all, she and Mary Rose hadn't wanted to come to the museum. It had been their father's idea. And it wasn't the greatest idea he'd ever had, Jo-Beth thought with resentment. Now, if he had arranged for a helicopter ride, or a trip in a hot air balloon . . . Jo-Beth closed her eyes and dreamed.

Mary Rose hadn't noticed. She was still outraged.

"I'm not leaving this place till I find that kid — "

Jo-Beth opened her eyes. "Boykin," she insisted.

"I don't care what you call him. He's still not a mannikin that's suddenly come to life. He's an ordinary kid, and somebody's put him up to all this now-you-see-me, now-you-don't fooling around."

Jo-Beth didn't want to hear anymore. She moved step by step to the exit and left.

Mary Rose noticed at last and ran after her.

Neither one spoke as they headed for the far side of the hangar. Then Jo-Beth caught sight of a sign on one of the trolleys. She stopped so abruptly that Mary Rose had walked on a little before she realized her sister wasn't at her side.

She turned, and demanded, "Now what?

First you can't wait to get back to Daddy, and now you've discovered something, haven't you?"

Jo-Beth just pointed to a sign on one of the trolleys.

Mary Rose sighed. Trust her sister to find a sign. It was Jo-Beth's ability to find signs that seemed to get them into trouble. When she read the sign, however, Mary Rose perked up. No way could a simple notice like this create a problem.

Hot Dogs and Lemonade — 5¢

The words had reminded Jo-Beth that she hadn't had anything to eat for a while. "I'm hungry," she announced. "I want a hot dog and lemonade."

"Who's going to give it to you? This place isn't even open yet."

"We won't know till we ask. I want a hot dog, Mary Rose." Jo-Beth dug into the pockets of her jeans. They were empty.

"I don't have a nickel. I don't have any money at all," she complained. "Lend me a nickel, Mary Rose, and I'll pay you back when we get home."

Mary Rose was about to refuse, then

thought better of it. Their father usually visited new places the day before they opened. If that was so now, then of course there would be supplies in this food trolley.

She sniffed. No fragrant aroma of hot dogs filled the air. But if there were hot dogs, and a grill they could turn on . . . her mouth began to water. Mr. Thorne wouldn't mind, she thought.

She found two dimes and a nickel in her back pocket.

"Okay, Jo-Beth. Come on. I'll treat, because it's your birthday."

"My birthday was yesterday," Jo-Beth began.

"I know," Mary Rose interrupted. "But you couldn't celebrate it yesterday because it was a school day, and the party isn't till tomorrow."

Jo-Beth felt a warm glow. She was the only one she knew who stretched out a birthday for three days.

This time the girls went into a trolley with nothing on their minds but food. Inside, the car was set up with a long griddle on one side, plastic cups heaped in a towering pile, and plastic knives and stirrers. Opposite the griddle was a long sliding window, which was shut tight.

Mary Rose searched the refrigerator at the far end. It was cold but empty. No rolls, no hot dogs. No food.

"We'll starve to death," Jo-Beth said in a gloomy voice. "Look how thin I'm getting."

Mary Rose ignored her. They had passed a huge popcorn machine near the entrance but had paid no attention.

"Will you settle for popcorn, if the machine is working?"

Jo-Beth's eyes gleamed. Popcorn! Terrific! "You've saved my life," she said. "I'm so hungry I could eat a mountain of popcorn."

"Wait. There's a sign, Mary Rose," Jo-Beth said when they reached the machine.

The sign urged customers to put a dime in the slot for coins, then wait a moment. A plastic cup would drop and would be held in place by two metal clips. Then popcorn would fill the cup.

Mary Rose dropped a dime in the slot. She waited. Nothing happened. She punched the slot hard with her fist. "Maybe the dime didn't fall all the way in," she explained.

Still nothing happened. With a scowl and tight lips that showed her impatience, she kicked the machine.

Jo-Beth was angry, too. "You dumb, stupid machine," she shouted. And she kicked it.

"Ouch!" said the machine. "That hurt! How would you like it if I kicked you?"

Jo-Beth jumped back.

"It *talked*. That machine talked."

Mary Rose glared at her. "Machines don't talk."

"This one did. You heard it. It must be a robot. Robots talk all the time — "

"This is not a robot. It's just a plain dumb popcorn machine. You put in a dime, popcorn comes out. That's it."

Mary Rose felt so frustrated, she lashed out at the machine again. She kicked it so hard, she could feel a streak of jagged pain shoot up her leg.

The machine whirred. The plastic cup dropped down. Popcorn poured out.

"See?" Mary Rose said.

Jo-Beth pulled the cup out when it was full, then stood helpless as more and more popcorn continued to flow.

"Stop it," she begged. "Get it to stop, Mary Rose."

Mary Rose was stricken with guilt.

"I think we broke it, Jo-Beth. We better get out of here."

The girls moved in haste to the exit. The popcorn spilled out and followed them.

Jo-Beth looked back and was chilled.

The machine was alive. It had to be. It had heard her say she could eat a mountain of popcorn, and that was what it was determined to do — create a mountain.

She could see what would happen next. The

popcorn would continue to gush out of the machine exactly the way porridge had flowed and flowed from the magic porridge bowl in a story she had read. Only that was a fairy tale. This was real. The popcorn would keep coming; she and Mary Rose would drown in it, and no one would ever find their bodies. The headlines in newspapers would scream "MYSTERY DEATHS IN TROLLEY OF DOOM."

Jo-Beth knew it was all her fault. But how was she to know this was a machine that granted wishes?

At the steps, Mary Rose slipped on some popcorn and fell, followed by Jo-Beth, who tumbled over her sister.

As they scrambled to their feet, two voices spoke at the same time.

"Are you hurt?" Mr. Onetree asked with concern.

"What do you girls think you're doing?" demanded Sam Thorne.

"We didn't mean to do it," Jo-Beth replied. "We kicked the machine, but we didn't know it was alive."

Mary Rose's eyes were aflame with anger when she took in the scene before her. Her father held the boykin's hand firmly. The boy-kin clutched his teddy bear against his chest and looked fearful. Sam Thorne had an iron grip on a bigger boy who also wore old-fashioned clothes from the park trolley. His brown eyes blazed with defiance. His short red hair bristled.

"Never mind the popcorn now," she said. She pointed her finger at the older boy. "I knew it. You didn't fool me for a minute. I knew there were two of you."

Sam Thorne gave her a sharp glance. "You know these kids?"

"No. I just knew somebody was trying to scare us out of our minds. After a while, I figured it had to be more than one person." She paused and frowned. "But I could never figure out why."

"Scared you?" Mr. Onetree glared at the older boy. "Scared you how?"

"I'd like to know *why*," Sam Thorne said with impatience. "And I'd like to know what you're doing here in the first place."

The older boy, who seemed to be about twelve, clamped his lips shut. He folded his arms. It was almost as if he had just shouted,

"I'm not talking. And you can't make me, either."

Sam Thorne studied the boy's obstinate expression. Then he shrugged. "Suit yourself, son. I'll just have to call the sheriff."

The boykin burst into tears, and begged, "Tell them, Tom. If you don't, I will."

"Don't say a word, Luke. They can't do anything to us. We're just kids," Tom said.

He turned and stared up at Sam Thorne. He knew that Sam Thorne meant what he said even before Thorne spoke again.

"Don't play games with me, young fellow. You explain, now, or I make that call. Clear?"

The boy fixed his gaze on Mary Rose. "I'm sorry — "

Jo-Beth broke in, "It had to be you, but we don't know how you did it."

"I can explain," the boy went on, as if Jo-Beth hadn't interrupted.

What he told them came as a surprise and a shock.

· 10 ·

The Two Best Girls in the World

Tom began, "We needed a place to stay, for a while anyway. We didn't expect to be here too long."

"I should hope not." Sam Thorne was annoyed. "What do you mean, you needed a place to stay? You're not wanted by the police, are you?" His voice was heavy with suspicion. "How come you picked my museum for a hiding place?"

"Just a minute," Mr. Onetree said. "Let's not leap to conclusions. Give the boy a chance to explain."

He put his hand on Sam Thorne's arm, as if to warn him to be silent.

Sam Thorne frowned but didn't speak.

Tom waited a moment to be sure, then picked up the thread of his explanation.

"Nobody is looking for us." He gave Sam Thorne an angry glance. "We haven't done anything wrong —"

The little boy, Luke, interrupted with impatience. "We came here because Daddy was feeling sick and we had no place else to go. We're homeless," he added.

Before anyone could comment, Tom said with a defiant air, "That's right. We're homeless. We've just been going from place to place so Dad could find some work somewhere — anywhere. But when he felt bad, I spotted this place, and we just came in —"

"Sneaked your way in, you mean." Hoot Turner had come up quietly behind the group and had listened before he interrupted.

"All right, then. Where's your father?" Sam Thorne asked. He looked around as if he expected the father to appear.

"We hid way back on the other side," Luke told them.

"If you ask me," Hoot Turner said, "you're just lazy, good-for-nothing —"

Mr. Onetree said, his voice sharp, "Stop right there, Hoot. You don't know anything about these boys or their dad. Let's not judge anybody until we have all the facts."

Jo-Beth gave a quick nod. Her father was always strict, but he was fair as well. He waited to hear your side of the story before he made up his mind what to say or do.

Hoot Turner glared at all of them. "I know one thing you don't. I bet these kids stole my doughnuts and milk."

He gave his head a positive shake, as if to say "Get around that if you can."

"We're not thieves," Tom said. His face had turned red.

"No? Well, all I can say is if you take something that belongs to somebody else, you're a thief. No two ways about it," Hoot Turner insisted.

"I didn't say we didn't take the food. We did. We were hungry. We gave half to my dad and Luke and I ate the rest. But we didn't steal it. We cleaned up your place, which was a mess — "

"I was going to get around to it," Hoot Turner explained in embarrassment to Sam Thorne.

"We gave you work for food." Tom turned to Mr. Onetree. "See, my father used to be an automobile mechanic in Detroit. Then they fired lots of the workers. Dad couldn't find a job. Things got so bad, we lost our house. So Dad decided we ought to head south — "

Mary Rose interrupted. "Where did you sleep if you didn't have a house?"

Tom lifted his chin, as if to dare her to comment when she heard his next sentence. "Out on the street."

"In cardboard boxes," Luke chimed in. He hugged his teddy bear harder. "And Tom found my teddy in a trash can and gave it to me. That wasn't stealing, was it?" he asked anxiously.

The girls stared at the two boys. They had often seen pictures of homeless people on TV, but they hadn't seemed like real people.

Sam Thorne shook his head. If he was touched by the story, he didn't show it. "Don't lie to me, young fellow. There are shelters for the homeless."

"Where do you go when the shelters are full up?" Tom asked. "My father decided if we had to sleep outdoors, we better head south where it's warm."

Luke took up the story. "Daddy tried so

hard to find a job. Finally he was so desperate he made a sign, *Will Work for Food*. Then he stood on different corners near stores."

Tom's voice was grim. "Mostly people just hurried or drove by. Dad used to say, 'They think I'm just a drunken bum, too lazy to work.'" Tom glared at Hoot Turner. Then he went on, "Dad said he didn't blame them. 'Times like this,' Dad said, 'people are afraid. I can't say I blame them.' But I did. People should care."

Silence followed. No one seemed to know what to say. Then Jo-Beth asked, "Where's your mother? Don't you have a mother?"

"She ran away," Tom told her. "She decided she wanted to be a rock-and-roll singer. She has a great voice," he admitted. "She said she'd make pots of money and then she'd send for us."

"But she didn't, did she?" Mary Rose's voice was gentle.

"We never heard from her again."

"Of course we didn't, Tom," Luke said. "I bet she tried and tried, only she didn't know where we were. Because we've been moving around so much. But she'll find us some day, Tom. Just you wait and see."

"Sure she will, Luke." Tom stroked his brother's head. "Just like you say."

But his eyes, when he stared straight ahead, were hurt and angry.

Jo-Beth's own eyes began to fill with tears.

Before anyone in the group could speak, a voice said, "There's no need to share our private lives with strangers, Tom."

The man put his hand on Tom's shoulder. He stood tall and thin, his cheeks hollow, his dark eyes both furious and ashamed.

He spoke to Sam Thorne. "You've a right to know who we are. My name is Doug Lorry. My older son is Tom. He's twelve and a half. The boy with the teddy bear is my son Luke. He turned five yesterday."

"Your birthday?" Jo-Beth was amazed. "Yesterday was my birthday, too. But I'm eight. I'm going — " She stopped speaking abruptly. She had been about to say there would be a birthday party for her the next day. That would be cruel, for it was plain to see no one had celebrated Luke's birthday.

Doug Lorry went on, "I'm sorry about the boys borrowing the clothing from the mannikins in the trolley. But their own clothes were in rags. I promise you, when I find work, I'll pay whatever they cost. Meanwhile, we'll move on, of course. You'll find we haven't done any damage, or harmed anyone, or — "

"Wait," Mary Rose exclaimed. "What about us? We were being scared right out of our socks."

"That's right." Jo-Beth suddenly remembered to be angry.

"Just a minute," Mr. Onetree said. He looked at his daughters. "What's all this about being scared?"

The girls took turns telling about their experiences in the different trolleys. When they were done, all the adults turned accusing looks at the two boys. Their father was especially upset.

"What was the big idea?" Doug Lorry demanded.

"Listen, Dad. They were snooping around, going from trolley to trolley. I was afraid they would find you . . . us. I just wanted to scare them back to their father," Tom admitted.

"You scared us all right." Mary Rose was enraged, remembering the funeral car and the voice from the coffin. "Why did you play that trick with the teddy bear on us?"

"It was so weird," Jo-Beth added, "that voice crying in the coffin. Crying and calling for help."

Even though she now knew it was all a trick, it still made her feel creepy.

"I kept trying and trying to keep you from finding us," Tom explained. "But you just didn't quit. You sure have guts." He looked at Mary Rose as he spoke. "I expected you to pass out. But you didn't."

Hoot Turner broke in. "What did you think you were doing when you pulled that 'H— o — o — t. H — o — o — t. You have been warned. B — e — w — a — r — e' stuff?"

"I just wanted to be sure you would stay away from the back of the building, where Dad was resting."

Doug Lorry looked grim. "There was no call for that, Tom. No call at all."

"It served them right," Luke piped up. "They stole my teddy."

When the girls protested, Mr. Onetree held up his hand, like a traffic cop on a busy intersection. "Let's not squabble. Tom, you say you were responsible for the voices they heard?"

"Tom's a ventriloquist." Luke stumbled over the word. "He's real good, except you can see his lips move."

"A ventriloquist?" Mary Rose couldn't believe it. "How can you be a ventriloquist if you're only twelve and a half?"

Doug Lorry explained, "We had a neighbor back in Detroit, an old-timer in vaudeville. He was a magician and a ventriloquist. He liked Tom, and when he saw that Tom was interested, he taught him how to throw his voice."

Mary Rose was fascinated. She forgot about her anger. "Can you show us how you do it?"

Tom grinned. "Sure."

In a moment, a voice seemed to come from Luke's teddy bear. "H — o — o — t. You have been warned. B — e — w — a — r — e."

"You moved your lips," Luke said.

"Yes, you did," Jo-Beth agreed. "I was watching."

"Okay, boys. It's time to pull up stakes," Doug Lorry said. "Let's go."

"Wait," Mary Rose cried. "Mr. Thorne, I've just had a great idea. This is such a big place. You're probably going to need a lot of help when you open the museum."

"Yes." Jo-Beth was enthusiastic, too. "Mr. Lorry used to be an automobile mechanic. Maybe you have some broken trolleys he could fix or paint or clean or something."

Tom leaped in, his eyes anxious. "I could help, Mr. Thorne. Maybe entertain the kids that come with their parents if they begin to get bored. Help keep the place clean. Anything."

"You belong in school, young man," Sam Thorne replied.

"How can he go to school if they don't live anyplace?" Mary Rose wanted to know.

Jo-Beth was proud of her sister. What a sensible, understanding, and down-to-earth girl she could be. You sure could rely on her.

"Why not give them a chance?" Mr. Onetree agreed. "It might work out very well for you."

"Hey, listen," Sam Thorne protested. "I can't solve the problems of the homeless."

"Nobody can, at the moment," Mr. Onetree said sadly. "But you can lend a helping hand to one family — this family."

Sam Thorne thought about that for a moment. Then he asked Hoot Turner, "What do you think, Hoot? Could you use some help?"

"Need help? In a place this size? You better believe it. And the boys are honest," he added. "They cleaned my place so well I almost didn't recognize it."

"Okay," Sam Thorne told Doug Lorry. "We have a deal. Now don't start thanking me until you hear what I have to say. To begin with, you'll have to get a place to live in town. I'll advance the rent against the salary I'll be paying you. The boys will have to go to school — "

"Agreed," Doug Lorry said at once.

"Agreed," Tom echoed.

"And we've got to get these boys some real clothes . . ."

"So I won't have to be a dummy anymore," Luke said.

Tom hugged him. "Nobody better call you that when I'm around."

Jo-Beth had what she thought was a wonderful idea.

"Daddy. Why don't you write a column about all this? Don't you think people would be interested in finding out how a real homeless family feels?"

"If you do, don't mention my name," Sam Thorne said with haste. He winked at Jo-Beth. "Otherwise I think you've got something special to write about." He reached over to pat Jo-Beth's head. "This is one good kid you've got."

"Two," Mr. Onetree corrected as he put his arm around Mary Rose. "I've got the two best girls in the world."

·11·

A Happy Ending

Mary Rose was happy. She leaped into the front seat of the car and closed the door quietly. When her father looked at her, she gave him a broad smile.

Jo-Beth was happy, too. She was already in the back seat. "I feel good all over," she announced.

"Because we're finally going home now?" her father teased.

Jo-Beth nodded, but her thoughts were on what had happened before they were on their way home at last, back to the moment when her father had announced in the museum, "I say we all go out for lunch." He glanced at his watch. "A very late lunch, but I feel the need for food. All those in favor, say aye."

"Great idea," Sam Thorne had agreed at once, "except you're my guests. All of you." He waved his hand to include Doug Lorry and his sons.

Hoot Turner refused, reminding Sam Thorne that somebody had to stay behind and mind the store.

The Lorrys piled into Sam Thorne's pickup truck. The Onetrees followed in their car. On the way to town, Jo-Beth had a sudden idea.

"Daddy, can we stop at a five-and-ten? I'd like to buy Luke a birthday present. A real one. Not something out of a trash can." She paused, then added, "You'll have to lend me some money."

"Sometimes you're a real genius," Mary Rose said. "I didn't even think of it."

Jo-Beth couldn't believe she heard that. She felt puffed up with pride. Her very own sister, who always criticized her, had called her a real genius.

Mr. Onetree winked at her. "I agree."

"I'd like to buy something for Luke, too," Mary Rose went on. "And I think we should buy him a birthday cake. With candles he can blow out. I bet he's never done that."

"Two geniuses in the family," Mr. Onetree said. "How did I get so lucky?"

In the five-and-ten in town, Jo-Beth bought a thick coloring book. Mary Rose chose a large box of crayons and striped, twisted birthday candles in pink and blue and red and green. The next stop was the bakery. Here the girls had a hard time making a choice. Jo-Beth wanted the double-rich chocolate cake with marshmallow frosting. Mary Rose favored a lemon cake with coconut and banana icing.

While the girls argued, Mr. Onetree whispered to the woman behind the counter. She nodded, disappeared with both cakes, and came back in minutes to show the Onetrees what she had done. Each cake was now cut neatly in half. She then fitted two different halves together. Now there were two cakes, each one half double-rich chocolate with marshmallow frosting and one half lemon cake with coconut-banana icing.

Jo-Beth's eyes glowed. "Wow! I never ever saw a cake like this. I wish — "

Mary Rose laughed. She knew what her sister wished.

"You've got it, Jo-Beth. One cake is for Luke. The other one is for you. Right, Daddy?"

"When you're right, you're right," he told her.

In the restaurant, which turned out to be a small diner, the Lorrys were timid about ordering, then tried not to eat too fast or too much.

The girls looked at each other. The Lorrys acted as if they hadn't seen or tasted real food in a long, long time.

"Eat hearty," Sam Thorne urged them. "There's plenty more where that came from."

Finally, Tom put his fork down. "I can't eat another bite."

"Me, either," Luke piped up. "I'm stuffed."

"You mean you boys don't have room for a piece of birthday cake? Not even a very small piece?" Mr. Onetree asked.

The boys looked stunned when Mr. Onetree took the cake out of its box. Doug Lorry seemed close to tears.

"I can't thank you enough — " he began, but Mr. Onetree put his fingers to his lips.

"Shhh. It's candle-lighting time."

He let Jo-Beth light the candles. Luke watched, wide-eyed.

"Blow them out," Mary Rose said. "First make a wish, then blow."

"I wish nobody to be homeless," Luke said. "Is it all right to wish that?" he asked in an anxious voice.

"It's the best wish I ever heard," his father said. "Come on, Luke. Let's blow the candles out."

The boys found they did have room for cake after all.

Then everyone sang "Happy Birthday." Even the few people sitting at the counter joined in.

"Oh, my," Mary Rose said, after a while. "I don't think I can move. I ate too much cake."

"Me, too," Jo-Beth sighed. She glanced at Sam Thorne, then asked a question that had been on her mind for a while. "How come you have all those different displays in your trolleys?"

"Got to you, did they?" Sam Thorne's laugh was hearty. "Tell you how the idea came to me. My dad started the museum, and I got to love the trolleys as much as he did. The only problem was, very few people ever came to see them. I told my dad I wanted to do something about that, but he wouldn't listen."

Just like Mary Rose, Jo-Beth thought. Mary Rose didn't listen, either.

"My dad said he was only interested in people who came because they loved trolleys as much as we did," Sam Thorne went on.

Without thinking, he picked up a paper napkin, dipped it into his glass of water, then carefully wiped icing off Luke's lips and fingers.

"I'd been out to Disney World," he continued. "I enjoyed the mannikins that moved and talked. And I noticed everybody else around me responded, too. So I asked myself, why can't I do something like that in this museum? The kids would love it — "

"So would grown-ups," Mary Rose interrupted.

Sam Thorne nodded. "So little by little, I began to put displays in here and there. I wanted to give people a taste of history in a way that would get them really interested."

"But it isn't real history," Jo-Beth objected. "You have a trolley that's a *hearse*."

"That's real history, too, child. Some trolleys were sold to a South American country where they were used as hearses."

Jo-Beth's mouth dropped open. What a weird idea! She turned to see if Mary Rose agreed with her, but of course Mary Rose hadn't listened. She was deep in conversation with Tom Lorry.

"Can you really do magic?" she wanted to know.

"Some," he told her. "But I'm better at throwing my voice."

"I know," said Mary Rose.

Tom's face reddened. "I was afraid you'd find us."

"That's okay, Tom." To change the subject, Mary Rose begged, "Make the bear talk again."

Tom's eyes crinkled with mischief. "All right. Watch the bear."

Mary Rose turned. The teddy bear had been propped up against a large ketchup bottle on the table. His eyes seemed to be fastened on Mary Rose.

Then he spoke. "Never hit a ghost with a baseball bat."

Jo-Beth jumped.

Luke grabbed the bear and scolded, "I told you not to do that anymore."

Mary Rose giggled. "You moved your lips, Tom. I saw you."

"You weren't supposed to be looking at me," he protested.

After that, Sam Thorne took the Lorrys around town to find someplace for them to live. And the Onetrees headed for home.

In the car, the girls were quiet for a while. Mary Rose thought about Tom Lorry. He had promised to write to her. She wondered if he would keep his word.

In the back seat, Jo-Beth whispered something.

"What?" her father asked. "I can't hear you, Jo-Beth."

"I said I think that today is the best birthday I'll ever have in my whole entire life."

Mary Rose turned to stare at her. "Including being scared out of your socks, you mean?"

"Including." Jo-Beth was quite firm.

Well, she thought, maybe that wasn't exactly true. She hadn't liked the scariness one bit while it went on. But then, when the mystery was solved, it was like watching a scary movie that turned out fine at the end.

Now she remembered something. "When we got into the car to come to the trolley museum, Mary Rose was mad."

Her sister frowned. It seemed such a long time ago. "I was mad? What about?"

"About not going to Amy Beck's house. Amy Beck, your best friend, remember? You were mad because you wanted to see dumb old Jordan Beck."

While Jo-Beth spoke, Mary Rose's mind wandered. Tom Lorry had promised he would try to visit her sometime, too. All her friends would turn green with envy.

"Well?" Jo-Beth insisted. "Dumb old Jordan Beck?"

For a moment, Mary Rose was honestly puzzled. "Who?" she asked.

Mr. Onetree grinned. Then he winked at Jo-Beth. "See? Just like my Angelina. All Mary Rose needed was to find someone more interesting."

Mary Rose didn't enjoy being laughed at. "What about you, smarty?" she asked Jo-

Beth. "You were mad because you had to go to school on your birthday."

"Don't be silly, Mary Rose. Of course I had to go to school. Who do you think I am, the queen of England?"

Mr. Onetree began to whistle softly. Mary Rose rolled her eyes upward, then turned back in her seat and shook her head.

Jo-Beth tightened her seat belt and leaned back.

If she were queen of England, there would be no homeless people in her land. Not one. And everyone would have a birthday party. No exceptions. Everybody. And . . .

Jo-Beth closed her eyes, then suddenly opened them wide.

"Daddy," she cried. "Did we have a happy ending?"

"You bet," he replied.

Jo-Beth sighed with relief. She sure did love happy endings.

APPLE® PAPERBACKS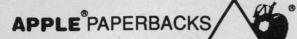

Pick an Apple and Polish Off Some Great Reading!

BEST-SELLING APPLE TITLES

☐ MT43944-8 **Afternoon of the Elves** Janet Taylor Lisle — $2.75

☐ MT43109-9 **Boys Are Yucko** Anna Grossnickle Hines — $2.95

☐ MT43473-X **The Broccoli Tapes** Jan Slepian — $2.95

☐ MT40961-1 **Chocolate Covered Ants** Stephen Manes — $2.95

☐ MT45436-6 **Cousins** Virginia Hamilton — $2.95

☐ MT44036-5 **George Washington's Socks** Elvira Woodruff — $2.95

☐ MT45244-4 **Ghost Cadet** Elaine Marie Alphin — $2.95

☐ MT44351-8 **Help! I'm a Prisoner in the Library** Eth Clifford — $2.95

☐ MT43618-X **Me and Katie (The Pest)** Ann M. Martin — $2.95

☐ MT43030-0 **Shoebag** Mary James — $2.95

☐ MT46075-7 **Sixth Grade Secrets** Louis Sachar — $2.95

☐ MT42882-9 **Sixth Grade Sleepover** Eve Bunting — $2.95

☐ MT41732-0 **Too Many Murphys** Colleen O'Shaughnessy McKenna — $2.95

Available wherever you buy books, or use this order form.

Scholastic Inc., P.O. Box 7502, 2931 East McCarty Street, Jefferson City, MO 65102

Please send me the books I have checked above. I am enclosing $_____ (please add $2.00 to cover shipping and handling). Send check or money order — no cash or C.O.D.s please.

Name_____ Birthdate_____

Address _____

City_____ State/Zip _____

Please allow four to six weeks for delivery. Offer good in the U.S.A. only. Sorry, mail orders are not available to residents of Canada. Prices subject to change.

APP693

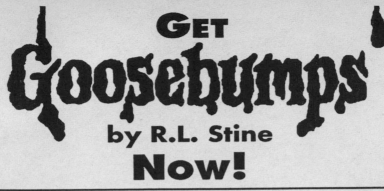

YOUNG
Robert
BURNS

CORBIE

Text by David Ross
Illustrated by John Marshall

© 1998 Waverley Books Ltd
Reprinted 1999

Published by Waverley Books Ltd,
New Lanark, Scotland

ISBN 1 902407 07 5

Printed and bound in Indonesia

YOUNG
ROBERT BURNS

Let us join young Robert Burns at his lessons. He is a very clever boy and he likes his lessons, most of the time. Two days a week the teacher comes to the little farmhouse where he and his young brothers and sisters live. Half a dozen children from the farms round about also squeeze into the small room. There are no desks, no blackboard. The teacher is a strong young man of eighteen, down from Glasgow University. With him they read, they write, they do counting. All this is fine for Robert, especially the reading and writing. He is better at these than any of the other children, and he is very good at remembering. His friends mostly prefer what comes next, the singing lesson. Their teacher, John Murdoch, has a fine voice and enjoys singing. He knows new songs from England, but Robert's father, who pays him, does not approve of modern songs and prefers him to teach the children to sing the old Scottish psalms.

At singing time, the other children relax. But Robert cannot sing. The tunes ring clearly in his head and tease him. He can hear them in his mind, but when he opens his mouth, only a dull flat drone comes out. And Robert is such a lively boy that John Murdoch does not

6

believe he can't sing. When it is Robert's turn to show that he has learned the words and tune, John quickly grows angry.

"The tune, sir," he calls. "You have the words but not the tune. Sing properly."

But it's no good. Robert can't sing.

"Very well," says his teacher, frowning heavily. "You know where the tawse is kept, I believe?"

All eyes watch Robert as he goes to where his father keeps the strap. Every house has one, and every house uses it. He hands it to his teacher.

"Now hold out your hand."

John Murdoch is a strong young man, and by the time he is finished Robert's hands are sore and swollen.

"Go and sit at the back. I have no patience for you."

His hands tenderly placed under his armpits, Robert retreats to the back row. Another pupil stands up to sing the verses.

At the end of the lessons, John Murdoch says goodbye before he walks the two miles back to Ayr, where he lives. His big hand ruffles the boy's dark hair.

"You're a good lad, Robin," he says. "You're quick at everything, bar one. But I'll make you a singer yet."

The boy gives him a rueful grin. At least there won't be any singing for another week.

he boy who could not sing grew up to give the world some of the most beautiful songs it has. Robert Burns, son of the poor farmer, was to become a great poet. But no one in his family expected this to happen. They expected Robin, as they called him, to grow up and become a farmer like his father.

Schooling took up only a little of young Robert's time. There was always plenty of work to be done about the farm. His father could not afford to pay anyone to help him. As the eldest son, Robert was expected to help, not just by doing a few odd jobs but by hard work every day. Between the ages of seven and eighteen, he lived on the farm at Mount Oliphant, two miles from Ayr. The soil was poor and did not produce good crops.

In springtime, when it was often cold, wet and windy, Robert helped with ploughing, walking behind the horse-drawn plough as it turned up the heavy ground. After ploughing, they harrowed to make the ground level and then sowed the seed. This meant carrying the seeds in a bag or on a tray and scattering it in handfuls, trying to spread it as evenly as possible. Hungry seagulls and crows would fly behind. Robert's brother

Gilbert, two years younger, would shout and wave his arms to scare them off the precious seed.

Sometimes Robert dreamed while he was at the plough. His strong arms held it steady, and his clumsy shoes tramped through the mud, but his mind was far away. He was telling himself stories or pretending he was someone else. But at other times his eyes were wide open and he saw everything around him very clearly. He saw the green hills and the trees and the cloudy skies. He had a sharp eye for little things. When a tiny mouse scrambled away as the plough pushed through its nest, he noticed it. He saw how the daisies came up and admired their beauty. His mind was open to wonder at the miracle of life in every form. He did not just look and think, "Oh, that's a daisy." To him, in that moment, it might be the loveliest and most surprising thing in the whole world:

"Wee, modest, crimson-tipped flow'r,
Thou's met me in an evil hour;
For I maun crush amang the stour
      Thy slender stem:
To spare thee now is past my pow'r,
      Thou bonnie gem."

CHAPTER THREE

Although they lived on a farm, the Burns family did not have a lot to eat. They could not afford beef or mutton. They mostly ate oatmeal, cheese and cabbage, and drank water, milk or weak beer. It was not a good diet for a growing boy, especially one who had to work as hard as Robert. At the end of the day there was no hot bath. There was no bathroom. The house had no taps or running water. All water was brought in a bucket from a well. There was no electric light – electric lighting was not yet known. The Burns family could only afford candles, one at a time. But as the evening darkened into night, Robert would sit reading by that single candle. There was no money to buy books, but they were able to borrow books from wealthier friends. The two books that excited young Robert most were the story of Hannibal and the story of William Wallace.

Hannibal was a great soldier of ancient times. During his life, Rome ruled the world, but Hannibal fought against Rome. His most famous deed was to lead his army, including elephants, across the snow-covered Alps into Italy. William Wallace was one of the greatest heroes of Robert's own country, Scotland. He had fought against the English King Edward the First to

keep Scotland a separate country with its own king. The story of Wallace made the boy fiercely proud that he too was Scottish. He read as much as he could about Scotland's history. In later years he wrote the famous song that begins:

"Scots, wha ha'e wi' Wallace bled,
Scots, wham Bruce has aften led,
Welcome to your gory bed,
*   Or to victory!"*

Robert dreamed of being a soldier. When the pipers and drummers came marching through, looking for young men to join the army, the little boy ran after them, wishing he was old enough to join. Perhaps, as he worked, the hills of Mount Oliphant became the mountainous Alps and his father's skinny horses became mighty elephants. Later in his life, when Britain was at war with France, he did indeed become a soldier. Like many others, he joined the Volunteers and was ready to defend his part of Scotland against the French.

Robert's father, William, was a quiet, gruff man. His mother, Agnes, was a busy farmer's wife, practical and thorough. She always had something to do, like milking the cows, making bread, mending clothes that were already worn-out, looking after her children – Robert was the eldest of seven. She was a good singer. She often sang as she worked, and he loved to hear her. His parents never knew what to make of this boy with the dark, sparkling eyes and ready laugh. Sometimes he would caper about like a lamb in the spring breeze, at other times it was impossible to get his attention away from a book. They did not have much time to spare for him. The person who did have time to spare was an old woman, a relation of his mother's, who sometimes came to help about the house and farmyard. Her name was Betty Davidson.

Betty was full of stories – the kind that children love

to hear. As Robert said later, her tales and songs were all about "devils, ghosts, fairies, brownies, witches, warlocks, spunkies, kelpies, elf-candles, dead-lights, wraiths," and so on. At night there were no lights outside but the moon and the stars, and no sound but the crying of the wind in trees and bushes. It was easy to believe that strange creatures moved in the dark. Tales that were pleasantly shivery in daytime could be terrifying at night. It may have been old Betty who first told him the story of Tam o' Shanter.

Tam o' Shanter was an Ayrshire farmer, like Robert's father, William. Unlike Robert's father, he enjoyed drinking and talking. One night he set off on his old grey mare, Meg, to return home from the inn. It was dark and late and his little farm was a long way off. The path led by the half-ruined church of Alloway, which was supposed to be haunted. As he approached the church, Tam was surprised to find it brightly lit. The ale he had drunk made him feel brave, and he crept up to take a closer look. What did he see?

Witches and warlocks in a dance! At one end sat the Devil himself, a great horned beast, playing the bagpipes so loudly that the walls shook. Most of the witches were ugly old women whom Tam could hardly bear to look at. But one was young and beautiful, and she danced more wildly than any of the others. At last she got so hot that she threw off all her clothes except a short smock, and she danced in that.

Tam could not restrain himself from calling out: "Weel done, Cutty Sark!"

And, in an instant, all was dark. Tam spurred his horse away, just in time. The whole band of demon revellers came pouring out in chase of him. Now it was time for his good grey mare to show how she could run. With the witches close behind him, Cutty Sark at their head, the terrified Tam galloped across the countryside. He was racing for a bridge. He knew that the witches could not cross running water and that he would be safe if he reached the other side. But even as Meg reached the centre of the bridge, Cutty Sark came racing up behind, stretched out her arm and snatched at Tam. But all she got was the old grey horse's tail. Tam had escaped!

How the boy's eyes shone when Betty told him such tales. He repeated them in a whisper to his brother, huddled in the narrow bed they shared, or silently to himself when his father shouted for silence, hugging himself with the excitement of the chase and the terror of the demon dancers. He knew his parents did not like Betty telling him her stories and that made him listen all the more, storing them up in his mind.

CHAPTER FOUR

John Murdoch, their teacher, got a new job teaching in the grammar school at Ayr and no longer tramped out to teach the country children. He did not forget Robert, however, and invited the boy to come to him for lessons. Robert walked to the town, and home again, and learned all he could.

Life was not quite all farm work, school and reading. There was time in the long summer evenings to play. Everybody knew everybody else, and children ran far and wide across the countryside. Robert's friends might include the children of the minister, or of a farmer with a bigger farm than Mount Oliphant, but as he grew older Robert found there was a difference between some of these children and himself.

"When you're a man, what will you be?"

"A soldier!" used to be young Robert's reply, but now his friends were old enough to think of a real career.

"I'm going to Edinburgh to learn how to be a doctor."

"I'm going to the university in Glasgow. My daddy wants me to be a lawyer."

Now Robert Burns had nothing to say. He was not going anywhere. When these boys went off to university, he knew he would still be at home. His

father had no money. He needed Robert's help with the farm. When these boys were doctors and lawyers, with big houses of their own and plenty of money, Robert Burns would still be a poor farmer, following the plough.

And he was so hungry to learn. He wanted to go to university and read more books. He wanted to learn French and Latin. His mind was itching with questions to which nobody around had an answer. Nobody even wanted to discuss them.

And then, one day, his playmates were gone, but when they came back it was worse. He saw his friend, just back from Edinburgh University, come riding along the track with another youth, a visitor from Edinburgh.

"Hello there!" called Robert, taking off his bonnet and waving it. They rode by, hardly even looking at him.

"Who's that?" asked the visitor.

"Oh, no one. One of the peasants from hereabouts. He probably wanted a penny."

Robert Burns felt that life was very unfair, not just to him but to many others like him, but there was nothing a teenage boy could do about it. He did not give up reading and trying to learn. Sometimes, at the dinner table, the whole family, father and children, sat reading books, hardly noticing what they were eating. The only exception was Robert's mother. She had never learned to read.

CHAPTER FIVE

When he was fifteen, Robert found he could write rhymes. At harvest time the farmers all helped one another, moving from one little farm to the next to cut the oats and barley. All the country children worked in the fields all day long. It was the usual thing to put a boy and a girl working together, the girl supposed to bundle the stems after they had been cut with the scythe, the boy supposed to do the heavier lifting. That summer, Robert's work partner was Nelly Kirkpatrick, a blacksmith's daughter. She was his first love. Later he wrote that she was "a bonnie, sweet, sonsie lass." To Nelly he wrote his first poem. It was the first of many that he wrote, to many different girls. Nelly was succeeded by Alison, Jean, Sophy, Bessy, Peggy, Nancy and others. In one of his songs, Robert wrote:

> *"The sweetest hours that e'er I spend,*
> *Are spent amang the lasses, O."*

Young Robert Burns had to stay at home, working on the farm. He still read books. But now, when he sat up late by candlelight, he was writing poems on whatever scraps of paper he could find. He wrote poems that

make us laugh, that make us cry, that make us sit down and think about ourselves and the sort of people we are. Above all, when he was still a very young man he wrote about love. One of his best-known love poems is this one:

"My love is like a red, red rose,
That's newly sprung in June;
My love is like a melody,
That's sweetly played in tune.

As fair art thou, my bonnie lass,
So deep in love am I;
And I will love thee still, my dear,
Till a' the seas gang dry.

Till a' the seas gang dry, my dear,
And the rocks melt wi' the sun!
O I will love thee still, my dear,
While the sands o' life shall run.

Soon his poems were read and recited by people round about. He was able to have them printed in a book, and he became famous in Scotland. After his death he became one of the most famous poets in the world, but he never became rich. His life had many ups and downs; he always had to work hard, and he was always short of money. Sometimes this made him feel sad and downcast, but usually he was cheerful, and he was always one of the kindest and most generous of men. He understood himself and once wrote:

"When sometimes by my labour I earn a little money, O,
Some unforeseen misfortune comes gen'rally upon me, O:
Mischance, mistake, or by neglect, or my good-natur'd
  folly, O —
But come what will, I've sworn it still, I'll ne'er be
  melancholy, O."